ROLEY

My Book

Aaron

Hi, I'm Roley.

I'm a big, green roller with heavy wheels. I'm good at flattening things like sand and gravel. I love music and I love rocking and rolling!

One day I was left to look after a sleeping hedgehog. It wasn't very easy…

All the machines were busy doing jobs.
There wasn't any rolling to do, so I was
waiting in the yard.

Then Scoop came rushing up, carrying
a box.

"What have you got there, Scoop?"
I asked.

Scoop lowered his front scoop and I peered into the box. A hedgehog was curled up inside.

"We found it in the old cottage," said Scoop. "It's gone to sleep for the winter. Bob says it's called hibernating and it mustn't be woken up."

Scoop asked me to look after it while he went to find Wendy.

I sang the hedgehog a rocking and rolling lullaby!

Pilchard heard me singing and came into the yard to see what I was doing. When she spotted the box, she stuck her paw in to see what was inside.

"**Waaagh!**" she howled.

"Careful, Pilchard!" I said. "Hedgehogs have very spiky prickles!"

Later, Farmer Pickles and Travis called round to see Wendy. I told them she was at the builders' yard.

"I'll go and find her there, then," said Farmer Pickles.

"Goodbye!" he called as he drove off. He didn't realise that Scruffty had jumped out of the trailer and was excitedly sniffing around the yard.

Scruffty crept up on Pilchard who was peeping into the hedgehog's box.

"**Ruff!**" he barked.

"**Miaooow!**" cried Pilchard. They started to chase each other around the yard. They ran round and round, knocking things over.

"**Stop!**" I shouted. "You'll wake up the hedgehog!"

But they just carried on.

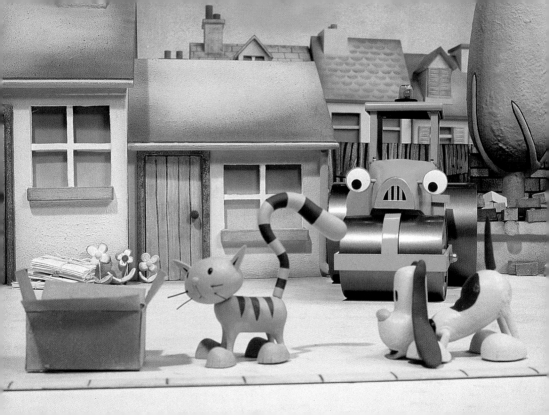

"Stop!" I shouted again. But Pilchard and Scruffty were making such a noise that they didn't hear me.

I went to get Farmer Pickles to help me. I rushed out to the countryside and told him all about the mess.

"Oh dear!" he said. "I'd better come and see what I can do."

When Farmer Pickles saw the mess he was very cross.

"Scruffty! Get into the trailer **now**!" he shouted.

Pilchard was very pleased that Scruffty was in trouble.

"You're just as much to blame," I told her. Then I checked on the hedgehog. Luckily it had slept through all the noise!

Farmer Pickles and I worked really hard clearing up the yard. Just as we finished, Wendy arrived back with Scoop and Muck.

"It seems very peaceful here," said Wendy. "Is the hedgehog still asleep?"

"Errr, yes…" I said.

Farmer Pickles and Wendy went to fix a gate in one of Farmer Pickles's fields.

"Let's play a game of football!" Muck said when they'd gone.

He passed the ball to Scoop.

"**Stop!**" I yelled as the ball bounced near the box. "You can't play here. You'll wake the hedgehog!"

It wasn't easy looking after a hedgehog!

When Bob and Wendy finally came back to the yard they found Scoop watching over the hedgehog.

"It's fast asleep," whispered Bob.

"Look! Someone else is fast asleep," said Wendy.

"Roley's hibernating,
too," said Bob.
"I wonder why he's
so tired?" said Wendy.
"It's not as if he's
had a busy day!"

"**Zzzzzzzzz!**"

I snored.

THE END!